GO FOR IT

GO FOR IT

THE PURSUIT OF THE ZYEGOAT

Qzye View

Zyetopia Publishing

First Edition, 2026

Published by Zyetopia Publishing
zyetopia.com
For permissions or inquiries:
info@zyetopia.com

ISBN (Paperback): 979-8-9954575-0-3
ISBN (Hardcover): 979-8-9954575-1-0
ISBN (Ebook): 979-8-9954575-2-7

To those who feel buried.

May Zye blossom.

Contents

INTO THE DARKNESS

The Dormant Seed

Weight. That is all you are.

It presses from every side—cold, wet, unyielding.

You can't tell if it's earth or fear. It smells of time. Of endings. Of beginnings that never began.

You try to move, but the motion is small—swallowed by soil.
It makes the faintest sound—a sigh pressed through dirt—
your first act against the silence.

Deep within, a single pulse stirs. At first, it seems foreign,
like the echo of someone else's heartbeat.

But as you listen, you understand: it's your own.

"You have been here a long time."

No voice speaks, yet the words arrive. They ripple through you like distant thunder—not heard but felt.

You want to respond, but you have not yet learned how.

So you reach.

Out to the left, the earth is compacted by old pressure and stone. To the right, it's softer—deceptive, as if it might swallow you the moment you trust it. Below, the darkness has no floor.

But above—so faint you cannot be certain—a difference. Not warmth. The absence of cold. A thinning in the weight, as if one direction is fractionally less absolute than every other.

You can't see it. You can't name it. You're not even sure it's real.

You reach toward it anyway.

Every direction is resistance. Every inch costs breath you cannot spare.

The soil gives a fraction. A tiny loosening.

Then it tightens again, as if correcting your audacity.

It surrounds you, reclaims you, presses the world back into your skin.

The thinning vanishes. The cold is even on all sides again.

You freeze.

And in the freeze, you feel it.

A hum beneath the silence. Something vast below you, like the breath of a sleeping mountain.

The rhythm grows until it becomes a pulse. At first, it terrifies you. Then it fascinates you.

You count its beats: one for fear, one for curiosity, one for hope.

You try again. Your reaching is clumsy—ugly—but it's yours.

You press outward. Not a creature with hands. A seed with roots, searching blind for water.

The soil shifts. The thinning returns—closer now, or you're closer to it. A faint gradient against your scalp, so slight it could be your own body heat reflecting back.

But it's enough. Direction is enough when it's all you have.

Cool air slips in—barely a thread's worth, and gone before you can be certain it was real.

You taste it. And the taste fills your mouth with something unbearable—open sky you have never seen.

"Do you hear it too?"

A whisper—soft, trembling—arrives from beside you. Perhaps, another seed, buried close, pressing against the same weight.

You can't see it. But you feel it straining, the way you feel your own pulse in your wrists. Its rhythm is so close to yours that for a moment you can't tell where your effort ends and its begins. As if the darkness beside you is holding a version of yourself you have not yet outgrown.

You want to answer, but the darkness presses closer.

You push anyway.

The earth groans—not loud, but deep, as if it has opinions about your existence.

The soil loosens. Then collapses.

It pours around you like a slow avalanche, filling every inch you fought for, as if the space had never belonged to you.

No air. Only pressure. Your mouth fills with grit.

For a heartbeat, you're certain you've lost.

Then the hum returns. Not above you. Within you.

Heat trickles into your chest—a spark too small to name, too bright to ignore.

It presses against your ribs like a memory you never lived. And it whispers not in words, but in meaning:

You are not buried. You are planted.

Something loosens. Not the soil.

You.

You stretch—awkward, slow—into the shape of yourself for the first time.

Each motion burns. Each inch costs breath.

But for the first time, you feel the specific pain of being alive. It runs along your joints like fire remembering how to move.

You reach upward.

A crack appears above you. Thin as a thread. Bright enough to blind.

Light threads through. For an instant—movement. The curve of sky. The pressure of wind. A voice you almost recognize.

The hum and your heartbeat synchronize.

You know nothing of what waits above. But your heart yearns. And the thought comes without asking: if you stay, the darkness will close back in.

You gather your will. You push.

The earth groans. The crack widens. Light spills through.

The presence returns—closer now, almost within your breath:

Rise. Rise and remember.

The soil collapses around you as you reach upward—and for a single breath, your face meets open air.

Wind cuts across your skin.

Then the earth shifts, dragging you back by inches.

But the crack remains.

The other seed calls out—faint now, falling behind you, its voice thinning with distance:

"Don't leave me here."

Your chest tightens. You reach back toward the dark. Your fingers brush soil. You find nothing.

The wind above pulls at your face. The earth below grips your ribs.

You hang between them—half-free, half-buried—and you cannot hold both directions.

You choose the crack.

The soil closes over the place where the voice was. The silence that follows weighs on your heart.

You do not look down again.

Above you, the crack holds. Below, the dark hums—patient, unchanged, waiting for the next seed to press against it.

And inside your chest, a sound so quiet it could be imagined:

The rhythm of something that has not yet learned it is alive.

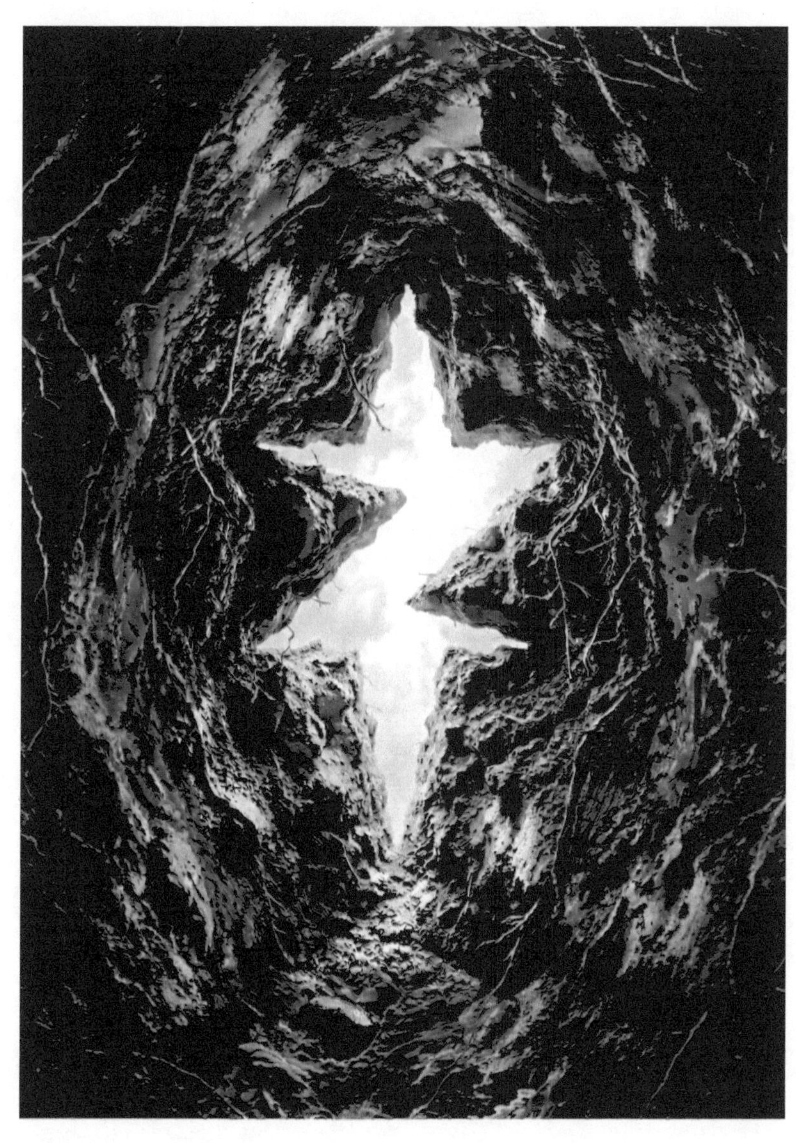

THE SPARK

The Call to Ascent

The first breath does not come easily. You tasted air once—a single stolen mouthful—and the earth tried to take it back.

Now you are half-held in the dark again. Your face pressed close to the crack. Your lungs remembering what they have always known.

Below you, the soil has closed over the place where the other voice was. You do not look down. But you feel the silence where it used to press against the earth beside you, and the silence has a shape, and the shape is absence.

Light seeps in—slow, then less slow, the way warmth returns to a numb hand. You feel it before you see it: a warmth above the soil, pulsing faintly. A heartbeat not your own.

The darkness loosens its grip. Your lungs widen.

You tilt toward the warmth. The soil shifts. Grains fall against your face like dry rain.

The air that enters smells foreign—cold, metallic, alive. It terrifies you.

Then, from beneath—faint, already fading:

"...hear it still?"

The voice is not beside you anymore. It rises through the soil like heat through stone, thinned by distance, already becoming memory. You can't tell if it's real or if your thoughts are echoing back at you.

Your throat tightens. You want to reach downward.

But downward is closed. Downward chose you, and you did not stay.

If you stop now, you make that choice meaningless.

You push upward.

The soil resists. Not gently. It resists the way a verdict does—heavy, final, unmoved by your reasons.

Each motion costs strength, but each brings a flicker of something you have no name for. It lives in the muscles, not the mind. It tastes like iron. It tastes like desire.

The crack widens. A ray of gold in the black.

For a moment, you freeze. The soil behind you is terrible—but oddly comforting. What you are climbing toward has no name and no promise.

The voice from below rises once more. Fainter. Almost nothing.

"Stay."

The word settles against the nape of your neck. The soil feels safe—the way a cage feels safe when the world outside is on fire.

But you have already chosen.

You press upward with everything left in you.

The earth groans. Splits.

Dirt fills your mouth. Your arms shake. Your chest locks tight. Panic fills the space behind your teeth, thick as soil—

And then the soil bursts apart in a cascade of dirt and light.

You emerge gasping into air that blinds you.

Wind rushes across your face, sharp and alive. Your eyes sting. Your skin flinches. Every nerve is waking at once, furious, overwhelmed.

Your hands slam into the dirt. You cough soil from the back of your throat—grit and iron and something older than you.

The spark inside your chest flickers. Small. Steady.

The earth still grips your waist, clinging like a hand that will not unclench. So you crawl—palms down, elbows scraping, fingers digging for purchase.

Dirt breaks loose in small avalanches. You pull. Your legs clear the edge. Your feet slide free with a wet, sucking sound—

And suddenly the ground is not holding you anymore.

It's beneath you.

You collapse, breathing hard, tasting air that burns.

Then you lift your head.

And there, at the horizon's edge, a mountain.

Its peak is lost in the clouds, but the shape is unmistakable—massive, inevitable.

It doesn't invite you. It doesn't threaten you. It simply stands. The way a question stands that has waited longer than you've been alive.

Something inside your chest tightens toward it. Not the spark. Something older. A recognition you can't explain—something in the bone, in the weight of you, that answers the weight of the mountain.

The hum that led you here deepens.

You place one foot beneath you. You push.

Your legs wobble. Your vision swims. The wind hits you full in the chest.

Still, you stand.

Dirt trickles from you in quiet streams. The last clinging grains slide away, and for the first time, nothing holds you up except yourself.

You breathe in—deep, ragged, yours.

The spark steadies.

You glance once more at the dark seam behind you—your former grave, your former shelter—and something beneath it pulls you, faint and familiar, like a heartbeat that is no longer yours.

You whisper:

"I was buried. Now..."

For a moment—brief, passing—you turn toward something that isn't the mountain or the soil. A direction you can't name, as if the air itself is gently pressing from within. Then it's gone, and the mountain fills your vision.

The hum inside you becomes a low, wordless chant: *Go. Go. Go.*

You take your first step.

Your foot strikes bare ground—hard, real, indifferent to your history.

Behind you, the crack in the earth remains. Thin as a needle. Steady as a pulse.

Ahead, the mountain waits—without urgency, without mercy, without the slightest interest in whether you arrive.

You walk toward it anyway.

THE FLAMEBEARER

The Discipline of Friction

The mountain looms, its slopes shimmering with ash and shadow, carved by winds older than memory.

Every step leaves a mark that the gust immediately erases—as though the path itself refuses permanence.

You walk anyway.

The spark in your chest fights the thin air, a pulse of warmth pushing against cold. You keep one hand pressed there to remind yourself it is real.

Your legs still tremble. Your joints ache as if they were forged too quickly. The soil is gone from your skin, but not from your memory. Neither is the silence where the other voice used to be.

The ground grows sharper beneath your feet. The air thins. The wind turns cruel.

It doesn't hit you once. It hits you again, and again—testing the edges of your resolve like stone against a blade.

You slip. Your hands catch you before your pride can.

Your palms scrape rock and grit. Friction burns along your skin.

You rise and keep moving.

Then—through the pale veil of fog ahead—you see light. Not sunlight. Firelight.

Small and steady, waiting.

You approach cautiously.

At the center of a clearing sits a wanderer cloaked in soot-colored cloth. Their face is hidden beneath the hood's shadow.

Before them burns a small flame in a bowl of stone. It dances without wind—calm and contained—obeying a law you have never been taught.

The wanderer does not look up when you arrive. Their voice is low, and every word lands like a strike of iron on cold steel.

"You made it through the soil."

A pause. Then:

"What did you leave there?"

The question stops you mid-step.

You open your mouth. Nothing comes.

The wanderer waits. The flame waits. The mountain waits.

You feel the answer in your chest before you can shape it into words—the voice calling "don't leave me here," the soil closing, the silence that followed.

"Someone," you say. The word scrapes coming out.

The wanderer nods once. Not with sympathy. With recognition.

"Good. Now you know what fire costs."

They gesture toward the flame. Without thinking, you kneel beside it.

Heat touches your face. It breathes in rhythm with your own breath, as if it recognizes what you carry.

The wanderer's hands rest on their knees. Scarred. Steady. The scars are not wounds. They are grooves, worn deep—the kind water makes in stone.

They nod toward a pile of dry reeds beside you.

"Build it again."

You hesitate. "I don't know how."

"That is why you are here."

Before you can protest, they extinguish the bowl with a swift motion, crushing the ember beneath a fistful of dust.

Darkness reclaims the clearing. Only the wind remains.

The loss hits you harder than it should. Not the fire—the certainty. You were borrowing it without knowing.

"Build it," the wanderer says from the dark.

You begin gathering reeds, fumbling in the dimness. Your fingers are clumsy. The pieces break. Your hands shake.

You stack the reeds the way you think they should be stacked—too tight, too desperate, too impatient.

You strike stone against stone.

Nothing.

Again.

Nothing.

Frustration rises in you like smoke with no flame to justify it. Your hands cramp. Your shoulders lock. Your breath turns sharp and shallow, the way it turned in the soil when the earth pressed back.

You are gripping the world again. You can feel it—the same strangling hold, the same desperation, as if force alone could make something live.

"Why can't I do this?" The words come out cracked.

The wanderer's voice arrives from the darkness, unhurried.

"Look at your hands."

You look. Even in the dimness, you can see them: white-knuckled, trembling, clenched around the striking stones as if trying to crush fire out of them.

"You hold everything like that," the wanderer says. "Stone. Air. *People*."

Your grip loosens. Not because you chose to. Because the word found the bruise.

"Try again," the wanderer says. "But this time, leave room for what you cannot control."

You exhale. Long. Shaky. Your shoulders drop a fraction.

You rebuild. Looser. Not careless—patient. You make a nest instead of a fist. You leave gaps where air can enter.

You strike again.

A spark leaps. Lands deep in the reeds.

It glows. Barely. A fragile ember smaller than your thumbnail, trembling as if unsure whether it wants to exist.

Your hands hover around it.

Everything in you wants to close your fingers over it. To protect it completely. To own it so thoroughly that nothing—not wind, not cold, not the mountain—can take it from you.

You cup your hands just enough to shield the ember. Not enough to suffocate it.

You give it air. You give it time.

The ember trembles. Steadies.

A thin tongue of flame rises.

Warmth spills across your palms. Your face softens. Your eyes sting, and you do not wipe them.

The wanderer watches for a long time before speaking.

"You did not create that," they say. "You made space for it."

The flame grows stronger, fed by your patience and the air you chose not to hoard.

The wanderer reaches into the coals and lifts a live ember with bare fingers.

You flinch. They do not.

They wrap it in black cloth and hold it toward you.

"Take it."

You stare at it. The cloth is already warm. You can feel the heat from a hand's width away.

"It will die," you whisper.

"Yes."

"And when it does," the wanderer says, "you will have nothing but your hands and the memory of what warmth felt like. And you will have to decide if that memory is enough to begin again."

They press the wrapped ember into your palms.

It pulses against your skin like a second heartbeat—smaller, hotter, more fragile than your own.

You hold it close to your chest.

The wanderer rises. For the first time, you see their full height—taller than you expected, leaner, as though the mountain has been sharpening them.

They turn their back to you.

"Wait," you say.

They stop but do not turn.

"How many times have you built it again?"

Silence. The wind moves through the clearing. The flame in the bowl—the one you built—bends and recovers, bends and recovers.

"I stopped counting," says the wanderer.

They walk into the fog without looking back.

The clearing empties. The wind returns to its full voice.

You are alone with the fire you built and the ember you were given and the silence where a teacher stood.

You look down at your hands—raw, trembling, lined with soot in the creases.

They look like the wanderer's hands.

Not yet as scarred. But the same shape. The same willingness to open.

And for a breath, the opening feels like more than a gesture. It feels like a direction—as if your palms, uncurled, are facing something your eyes cannot find. Not the mountain. Not the path. Something the hands know that the legs have not yet learned.

Then you stand. You tuck the ember beneath your cloak, close to your heart.

The flame in the bowl gutters once, recovers, then burns on without you.

You step back onto the path.

The climb does not feel easier. Your legs shake. The wind sharpens. The cold presses in as if it has been waiting for you to leave the clearing.

But beneath your cloak, the ember pulses.

And your hands—though they ache, though they tremble—know now what they did not know before:

how to open when everything in them wants to close.

THE STORM

The Price of Heat

The ember's warmth is the only part of you that doesn't ache.

The higher you go, the quieter the world becomes. Not peaceful—just thin.

The air loses its softness. Sound loses its warmth. Even your breath feels sharper, as if it is scraping its way in.

The mountain does not welcome you. It watches.

Every ledge feels like a question. Every incline feels like a dare.

You keep moving.

The ember wrapped in black cloth rests against your chest—a second heartbeat beneath your ribs. Sometimes you press your palm to it just to remember that you can carry warmth.

But the mountain tests that belief quickly.

The sky shifts. Clouds gather without warning, swallowing the pale sun. Wind rises in a single, sudden surge—violent, impatient—and the temperature drops as if the world has turned its back on you.

Snow begins to fall.

At first it is gentle. Almost beautiful. Then it thickens.

Each flake draws a thin line of cold across your skin. The wind does not push—it presses, steady and deliberate, like a hand against your mouth.

Your ears go numb. Your cheeks burn, then vanish into cold. The path disappears beneath white.

You squint into the storm and see nothing. The mountain is erasing the road as you watch.

You slow. Not because you want to, but because your body demands it.

Your legs burn with fatigue. Your calves cramp. Your lungs ache as they fight for each inhale.

The spark in your chest flickers. Not from weakness—from pressure.

You tighten your cloak. You keep going.

The wind hits you sideways and you stumble. You catch yourself on rock, and your hand slices across ice. Your palm splits open. Blood beads, then freezes before it can fall.

You clench your jaw and move again.

The mountain does not care. It simply is. And you are the one who chose to meet it.

Snow thickens into a wall. The world shrinks to your next step. Your next breath. Your next refusal to stop.

Then—through the howl of wind—you hear it.

Stay.

Not a stranger's voice. You know this voice. You have carried the shape of it since the soil—the trembling, the fading, the sound of someone you could not hold calling after you as the earth closed between you.

Stay. Come back down. It's warm where I am. It's quiet.

Your feet slow. Your shoulders curl inward.

You nearly believe it. Not because it makes sense—but because exhaustion makes everything sound wise.

You imagine warmth below. Rest. The soil receiving you without judgment.

You imagine being buried again and calling it peace.

Then you feel the ember against your chest—and the memory that breaks through is not the wanderer's lesson.

It is the sound of the soil closing over the place where the voice was.

You kept climbing then. You left someone in the dark to do it.

You keep going.

The storm grows crueler.

Your vision blurs with snow. Your fingers stiffen. Your shoulders lock.

The wind steals your breath mid-inhale and you gag, lungs spasming as cold air cuts through you like a blade turned sideways.

Your hand goes to the black cloth. The ember.

You pull it out with shaking fingers, huddling behind a jagged rock that offers only partial mercy.

You unwrap the cloth.

The coal glows faintly—a single stubborn eye staring back at you from the dark.

You cup your palms around it and breathe—slow, careful. Warm air from your lungs meets the coal and the glow deepens. For one breath, you believe it will hold.

The wind finds the gap between the boulders. It slides through like a finger finding the gap in armor.

The glow flickers.

You tighten your hands. Your fingers press so hard they whiten. You are holding the ember the way you hold everything—too tight, too desperate, as if grip alone could keep warmth alive.

The wanderer's voice surfaces in your memory:
You hold everything like that.

Another gust. The coal dims to gray at its edges.

You bring it closer. Your lips nearly touch the cloth. You breathe into it the way you would breathe life into something drowning—everything you have, everything you are.

It comes once more—not a gust but a long, deliberate exhalation, as if the mountain itself is blowing out a candle.

The ember dies.

The glow shrinks to a point, lingers for half a second as if deciding—then vanishes.

Your hands stay cupped around nothing. The cloth is warm for three more heartbeats. Then it is not.

You kneel in the snow behind the rock and hold the dead weight against your chest.

Cold enters through your palms. Your wrists. The long bones of your arms. Following your blood back toward your heart.

The spark in your chest—the first one, the one that was yours before the wanderer gave you anything—dims. Not from wind. From grief.

You look at the black cloth. You look at the snow. You measure the distance between kneeling and lying down.

It is very short.

The voice returns. Softer now. Almost tender.

You tried. It is enough. Come down. Come back to the quiet.

Your knees soften. Your spine curves. Your chin drops to your chest.

Cold begins to crawl into your thighs, slow and heavy, like something claiming territory it has always owned.

Your eyelids lower. Just one breath without fighting, you think. Just one moment without deciding anything.

The snow receives your weight without objection.

And for a moment, beneath the cold, you feel it—a rhythm pressing against the earth below you, faint and familiar, as if the ground remembers the shape of you before you rose from it.

And then—beneath the storm, beneath the grief, beneath the old familiar pull toward sleep—

A pulse.

Small. Unimpressed by the weather.

Not warmth. Just rhythm. The same rhythm you counted in the soil: one for fear. One for curiosity.

You wait.

It comes.

One for the hands that remember.

Everything in you wants to stop. You start searching for structure.

The mountain gives you jagged stone and nothing else. So you use it.

You wedge yourself into the tight curve of two boulders where the wind cannot fully reach. You stack smaller rocks into a crude barrier. You pull loose splinters of dry brush from a crack in the stone—small, brittle gifts the mountain forgot to take back.

But your hands are too numb to hold them. The brush slips from your grip. Your fingers have locked into stiff, useless hooks that cannot close around a striking stone.

You press your palms flat against your stomach beneath your cloak, trading core heat for dexterity—feeling the warmth leave your center and seep into your knuckles, your fingertips, the joints that must bend. By the time your hands can close, your chest is colder than it was before.

The barrier collapses.

You rebuild it. Not with patience this time. With stubbornness.

You press your forehead to the rock and let the storm roar past while you force your body to slow.

Then, with shaking hands, you strike stone against stone.

Nothing.

Again.

Nothing.

Your hands cramp. The cold has made your fingers into strangers. You cannot feel the striking stones—only the impact traveling up your wrists, and a bright wrongness in your left palm you cannot afford to think about.

You strike again.

A spark jumps. Briefly. Dies before it touches the brush.

You do not pause. You do not breathe a prayer. You do not wait for readiness.

You strike again. And again. And again.

A spark lands. Catches.

For half a heartbeat, a tiny ember glows in the brush.

You do not cup your hands gently this time. You throw your whole body over the nest, becoming a wall against the wind. Your cloak spreads. Your back takes the storm's full weight. Snow drives into your neck, your spine, the backs of your legs.

You breathe into the ember—not carefully, not beautifully—with the ragged, desperate breath of someone who has already watched fire die once tonight and will not watch it again.

The ember trembles. Flickers.

Holds.

A thin tongue of flame rises—smaller than the one in the clearing, uglier, less steady.

It does not matter. It is yours. You built it from nothing but what the wanderer said you would have: hands and memory.

You feed it slowly. Splinter by splinter. You shelter it with your body and let the cold have your back.

A small fire blooms between stone and breath.

Not comfort. Survival.

The storm still rages, but now it rages outside your circle of heat.

You press your hands toward the flame, trembling. The cold retreats inch by inch.

And in that fragile pocket of warmth, beneath the howl of wind, you hear your own heartbeat return to your ears.

You close your eyes.

Your body softens into the heat the way a fist softens when it forgets what it was holding.

The voice comes once more. Softer now. Almost gentle.

Stay.

You open your eyes and stare into the flame.

"No."

Not shouted. Not proud. Just a word—small and final.

You sit with the storm. You endure. You shelter your fire.

Hour by hour, the wind loses its rage. The snowfall thins. The sky lightens from black to deep gray.

Then, slowly, dawn bleeds into the clouds.

The storm releases you. Not because you earned kindness—but because you survived its trial.

You stand—stiff, aching, alive.

You stamp out what remains of the fire. The coals hiss against the snow and send up a thin ribbon of smoke that the wind carries away before it can rise.

Your hands are cracked. Your face is raw. Your body is heavy with the kind of tiredness that lives in the marrow, not the muscles.

But inside your chest, the spark burns steadier than before.

You step out onto the path the storm tried to erase.

The mountain rises above you, still waiting.

You look down at your hands. The soot from last night has mixed with blood from your split palm. The lines in your skin are darker now, deeper—as if the mountain is writing something into you that you will not be able to read until much later.

You take one step. Then another.

The wind is quiet for the first time in hours. Snow covers the path ahead in unbroken white.

No footprints. No marks. No proof that anyone has ever climbed this high.

You set your foot into the blank snow and leave the first track.

Behind you, where the fire was, a faint scorch mark darkens the stone—too small to see from the path, too stubborn for the snow to cover completely.

THE PASSAGE

What the Hands Refused

The path narrows after the storm.

Rock walls rise on each side, pressing the sky into a thin band of gray above you. The wind cannot reach you here. The silence feels borrowed.

Your hands still ache from last night. The soot-and-blood lines in your palms have dried dark. You walk with your fists half-closed, protecting skin that is no longer bleeding but has not yet healed.

The ember is gone. You carry nothing now but the spark in your chest and the memory of how to strike stone against stone.

It should feel like enough.

It does not.

Every few steps, your hand drifts to the place beneath your cloak where the ember used to rest. Each time, your fingers find only cloth.

You are so occupied with what you have lost that you almost miss what is ahead.

A shape on the path. Low. Still.

You slow.

A figure lies against the rock wall, half-propped, half-collapsed—another climber, smaller than you, curled inward the way you curled behind the boulders last night.

Their cloak is thinner. Their hands are bare, palms open—not reaching, not gripping, just open, the way hands open when the body has stopped deciding what to hold. Their skin has the gray-blue pallor of someone the cold has already begun to claim.

They are shaking. Not the violent trembling of a body fighting—the slow, shallow shudder of a body forgetting how.

You stop three paces away.

Their eyes find you. They do not speak.

The look is one you recognize. You wore it behind the boulders, in the snow, with the dead coal pressed against your chest. It is the look of someone measuring the distance between kneeling and lying down.

You know what they need. You know because you needed it twelve hours ago: warmth, shelter, another body between them and the wind. Hands that know how to build a fire.

Your hands know.

And beneath the knowing, an older recognition stirs—the shape of someone slumped against earth, reaching, the voice you left in the soil now wearing a different body.

You look down at your hands.

The left palm is split from the wrist to the base of the fingers—the ice-cut from the storm, opened further by the striking stones. The edges of the wound are white and hard, pulled apart by cold. You cannot fully close that hand. When you try, the skin stretches and a bright, clean pain shoots to your elbow.

Your right hand is better, but not by much. The fingers are swollen at the knuckles, stiff from hours of gripping in the cold. You can feel your pulse in the tips—a dull, numb throbbing, as if the blood cannot decide whether to stay or retreat.

You try to curl your fingers around an imaginary stone. The motion is slow, clumsy. Your grip has no strength. The hands that struck fire last night did so on the last fumes of something you have not yet replenished.

The passage is narrow. Stone is close. There is dry brush wedged in the cracks—you can see it from here, the same brittle gifts the mountain leaves in its crevices.

You could stop. You could kneel. You could try to strike stone against stone with hands that can barely close.

But your legs are trembling—not from emotion, from depletion. The muscles in your thighs have been shaking since dawn in a fine, involuntary vibration you cannot stop. Your breath is still too shallow. Your vision narrows at the edges when you turn your head too quickly, a gray curtain drawing in, reminding you how little you have eaten, how little you have slept, how close you came last night to not standing up at all.

You are not the person who sat beside the wanderer's fire with a full body and eager hands.

You are what the storm left.

And what the storm left is not enough. That is what you tell yourself. The thought arrives with the weight of fact: You cannot help them because there is nothing left to help with.

You barely kept yourself alive. You do not have a second fire in you. If you kneel here and fail—if the brush is too damp, if your hands cannot grip the stones, if the effort drains the last of what holds you upright—you will be the one lying against the wall. You will be the shape someone else walks past.

The logic is sound. The logic is perfect.

The logic does not explain why your chest tightens when the climber's eyes stay on you.

It does not explain why the spark—steady, still burning, no dimmer than it was an hour ago—presses against your ribs as if trying to get your attention.

You do not listen.

You lower your eyes.

You step around the figure the way water steps around a stone—without force, without acknowledgment, without changing direction enough to admit you made a choice.

You keep walking.

For ten steps, you feel nothing. The passage narrows further. Your footsteps echo.

Then, at the eleventh step, a sound reaches you from behind.

Not a word. Not a cry.

A breath. One long, rattling exhalation—the kind a body makes when it stops expecting anything.

You do not turn around.

Your hands clench at your sides. Not from cold. From something that does not yet have a name but sits in your chest like a stone swallowed whole.

You walk faster.

The passage opens into a wider corridor of rock. The sky expands. The wind returns, gentle now, brushing your face the way it did when you first emerged from the soil.

You should feel relief. The storm is behind you. The path continues.

But your hands will not unclench.

And somewhere behind you—in a narrow corridor of stone, against a cold wall, in a silence you chose not to break—someone is still shaking.

Or they're not.

You don't go back to find out.

THE MOUNTAIN SPIRIT

The Echoes Within

You have not unclenched your hands since the corridor.

You notice this the way you notice a held breath—only after it has gone on too long. Your fingers are locked, nails still pressed into your palms, and the crescent marks have deepened from pink to a dull, angry red.

You try to open them. Your hands resist, as if they have decided something your mind has not yet admitted.

You climb.

The path narrows. The air thins further. Below you, the world disappears into cloud.

The higher you go, the less you can rely on sight. So you begin to rely on something else.

Listening.

At first, you listen outward—for wind, for loose rock, for danger.

Then you notice the louder sound: yourself.

The scraping of your breath. The thud of your heartbeat. And beneath both, a silence that has a shape—the shape of a narrow corridor, a figure slumped against stone, a breath you heard at the eleventh step and kept walking.

You have not thought about it directly. You have walked faster instead. You have studied the path instead. You have pressed your hand to the spark in your chest and told yourself: *forward, forward, forward.*

But the body keeps what the mind refuses.

Your hands are still clenched.

You round a bend in the ridge and find a passage carved into stone. No sign marks it. No light guides you. Only a stillness so deep it feels alive.

You step inside.

The temperature changes immediately. The wind vanishes. The sound of the outside world shuts. Completely.

Your footsteps become thunder.

The corridor slopes downward, then levels out, leading you into a vast chamber of dark rock.

At its center, a single pool of water lies perfectly still. No ripple. No reflection. The water is holding its breath the way you have been holding yours.

You approach slowly, wary of breaking the quiet.

You kneel at its edge and look down.

You do not see your face.

You see hands.

Your hands—reflected in the dark water but closer than they should be, larger, every line of soot and dried blood visible. The split palm. The swollen knuckles. The creases where the mountain has been writing.

And beside them, another pair of hands. Bare. Blue-gray. Still.

The hands from the corridor.

Your stomach drops. You pull back from the edge.

The pool does not change. The image holds.

Then, from within you, a voice rises.

From the oldest room in your chest.

"You do not belong here."

The words land clean and familiar. You have heard them in rooms that smelled like dust and old paper. In postures held too long. In the particular silence of waiting for something bad to finish happening.

You swallow.

And the mountain begins to speak through your own echoes.

A second voice follows—sharp with exhaustion:

> *"You're already tired. You already proved enough. Why keep bleeding for a peak you may never reach?"*

A third voice—quiet, resigned:

> *"You will climb. You will fall. And the world will forget you climbed at all."*

Your jaw tightens. You recognize the voices not by what they say, but by how your body braces against them.

You want to argue. You want to fight them the way you fought the soil.

But the chamber holds you still, forcing a different truth: these are not intruders. They are yours. You have been carrying them like stones in your lungs.

You breathe. The first voice speaks again.

> *"You do not belong here."*

You don't deny it. You don't fight it.

"I am here," you say.

The words settle in your chest. Not triumph. Just fact.

The second voice rises:

"You're already tired. Why keep bleeding?"

Your body answers before your mouth can: your muscles have been shaking since the storm. Your hands are cracked. Your shoulders bow under the weight of the question, and you let them bow. You do not argue with what is true.

The third voice whispers:

"It won't matter. No one will remember."

Your throat tightens. The old pull toward disappearing tugs at the base of your skull. Your jaw clenches. Your feet do not move.

Your hands, open at your sides, begin to close—slowly, without permission, the way they closed in the corridor.

Silence follows. Not empty. A silence that listens.

Then a fourth voice comes.

It does not shout. It does not accuse. It does not crawl from the dark places.

It speaks from beside you—close, quiet, trembling.

Don't leave me here.

The air leaves your lungs.

You know this voice. You have carried the shape of it since the soil—the sound of something reaching for you as the earth closed between you.

Your hands, already fists at your sides, tighten until your nails press crescents into your palms.

Don't leave me here.

You open your mouth to answer, and nothing comes. The answer you gave the other voices—*I am here, I am tired, I will keep going*—does not fit this one.

The chamber waits.

Then a fifth voice arrives.

No words this time. Just a sound.

One long, rattling breath—the kind a body makes when it stops expecting anything.

It fills the chamber. You cannot escape it. You cannot argue with it.

Your knees weaken.

You want to speak—to explain, to justify. My hands were broken. I had nothing left. I could barely stand.

The words form behind your teeth. They are ready. They are reasonable.

But the pool is watching, and in the pool, your hands float beside the still, blue hands of the one you passed—and your hands do not look empty.

They look closed.

The spark in your chest presses against your ribs. Steady. The same steadiness it had in the corridor, when you chose not to listen.

You understand now what the spark was doing.

It was not warning you that you had too little.

It was telling you that you had enough.

You did not listen.

The chamber is very quiet.

You kneel at the edge of the pool with this knowledge sitting in your chest like a coal you cannot spit out and cannot swallow. Your breath comes shallow. Your eyes sting.

You do not cry because you are sad. You cry because you are accurate. You can see yourself clearly for the first time, and what you see is not a hero who endured. It is a person who endured and a person who walked past. Both in the same body, carried by the same hands.

The pool holds the image without judgment. It does not flinch. It does not comfort.

It reflects.

For a long time, you kneel there.

The echoes do not return. They have said what they came to say. The first three were old weather—doubt, exhaustion, insignificance. You have answered them before and you will answer them again.

But the fourth and fifth are new. They do not dissolve when you speak back to them. They are not doubts. They are debts. And debts do not quiet when you acknowledge them.

They quiet when you pay them.

The mountain presence moves through the chamber—not as voice this time, but as pressure. A vast attention, resting on you without weight, seeing without comment.

It waits.

You look at your hands reflected in the water. The split palm. The soot grooves. The nails still pressed into your own skin.

Slowly—muscle by muscle, joint by joint—you open them.

Your fingers uncurl. Your palms flatten against your thighs. The crescent marks from your nails fill with blood and sting.

It is not a grand gesture. No one sees it. The chamber does not brighten. The pool does not ripple.

But your hands are open.

And for the first time since the corridor, the spark in your chest does not have to press to be felt. It simply burns, the way it was always burning, steady and unimpressed—waiting for you to stop clenching around it.

The presence speaks once. Quietly. Not as comfort—as direction.

"Go higher. But do not go the same."

You rise.

Your legs are not steadier. Your breath is not calmer. Your body aches in every place it ached before.

But your hands are open.

Your legs carry you forward.

Your hands carry what you owe.

You glance into the pool one last time.

Your reflection has changed. Not your face—but the posture is different. The shoulders are lower. The fists are gone.

You look like someone who is carrying something heavy and has stopped pretending it is not there.

You turn and walk out of the chamber.

The wind greets you. The mountain remains immense.

But as you step onto the path, you notice your hands are still open at your sides—palms facing slightly outward, as if expecting nothing, refusing nothing, ready for whatever the mountain puts into them next.

Behind you, in the chamber, the pool settles into perfect stillness.

On its surface, for a moment, a reflection lingers that is not yours—a figure slumped against stone, breathing slowly, waiting.

Then the water goes dark.

THE THRESHOLD

What the Mountain Asks

Your palms are still soft from unclenching when the path steepens until it is no longer a path.

Rock gives way to dark stone, tilted upward at an angle your legs can barely hold. Your feet slip. Your hands reach for holds that are not there.

There is nothing left to grip.

You press your palms flat against the stone and push. The surface is cold and featureless—no crack, no ledge, no seam. Your fingers scrape uselessly. Your nails find nothing.

You have spent every stretch of this climb reaching, gripping, building. Your hands have been your answer to every question the mountain has asked.

The stone asks nothing. Your hands have no answer anyway.

You shift your weight and push again. Your split palm drags against the stone, and fresh blood smears across the rock in a thin, red line. The pain is bright and immediate.

You stop.

You lean into the stone to steady yourself. The incline has steepened without your noticing—what was a slope is now nearly vertical. Your weight presses against it, not climbing, just resting.

Your arms tremble. Your breath comes fast and shallow. The wind is thin up here, barely enough to carry sound, and the silence has a different quality—not the held-breath silence of the chamber, but the open silence of a place that has been empty for a very long time.

You look up.

The summit is close. You can feel it—not see it. The stone levels somewhere above you, no more than thirty steps if the path were flat. But the path is not flat. The path is a wall of smooth stone, and your hands cannot climb it.

Everything in you revolts.

You have come too far. You have paid too much. You survived the soil, the storm, the corridor, the chamber—and now the mountain says no with a surface that offers nothing to hold?

Your fists clench. The old reflex. Blood from the split warms the creases of your palm.

You strike the stone. Once. Hard. Open-palmed.

The sound is flat and final. It does not echo. The mountain absorbs it. Completely. Without acknowledgment.

Your hand stings. Your wrist aches. Nothing has changed.

You lean your forehead against the cold rock and breathe.

The spark in your chest burns. Steady. Untroubled. It does not need your effort to exist. It has never needed your effort to exist.

And you feel the full weight of that fear.

The wind passes over you—thin and indifferent.

You are not climbing. You are not falling. You are standing against a wall you cannot scale.

Something shifts in your chest. Not the spark—the space around it.

A loosening. Like a fist unclenching, but deeper—not in the hands. In the place behind the ribs where you have been gripping your own survival since the first moment you woke in the dark.

You do not decide to let go. The holding simply becomes too heavy to continue.

Your hands flatten against the stone. Not pushing. Not gripping. Just resting.

Your weight shifts backward. Your feet find a narrow ledge you did not notice before—or that was not there before. It does not matter which.

You lower yourself to your knees.

Not in defeat. Not in prayer.

In the only posture left.

You kneel on the ledge with your palms open on the stone and your forehead touching rock, and you stop.

You stop climbing.

You stop reaching.

You stop proving.

The wind moves over your back. Your cloak flutters once and settles.

For a long time—you do not know how long—nothing happens.

Your mind screams. It screams that this is surrender. That the mountain will close in. That the soil is waiting. That you have come this far only to kneel at the gate and be turned away.

Your body does not listen to your mind.

You breathe in. Slowly. The way you breathed into the ember—except this time, you are not trying to keep anything alive.

The stone beneath your palms grows warmer. Not from your heat—from something rising through the rock itself, a deep warmth, as if the mountain's own pulse has finally reached the surface.

The spark in your chest answers it. Not with a flare. With a steadying — brief, fragile, like a flame finding shelter it doesn't yet trust.

You breathe out.

And something leaves with that breath.

Not the spark. Not the grief. Not the debt.

The need to be climbing.

It lifts off your shoulders like a cloak you did not know you were wearing, and the cold that follows is sharp, immediate, and clean—the cold of standing unprotected in open air, without armor, without momentum, without the story of yourself as someone who must always be ascending.

You are no longer a climber.

You are someone kneeling on a mountain with open hands and no name for what comes next.

The stone levels beneath you. You do not feel the transition. One moment your knees are on the ledge; the next, the ground beneath them is flat—wide, smooth, ancient.

You raise your head.

The summit opens before you.

Not with banners. Not with light. Not with the voice of the mountain congratulating you.

With space.

A vast, bare plateau of dark stone, open to the sky on every side. No walls. No shelter. No path forward and no path back.

Only the wind. Only the stone. Only you.

You place your palms flat on the ground and push yourself upright.

Your legs shake. Your body sways.

You stand on the summit the way a newborn stands—unsteady, unburdened, uncertain of everything except the fact of being vertical.

The wind touches your face.

Behind you, somewhere on the smooth stone wall, a smear of blood dries in the cold air—your last act of gripping, already becoming part of the mountain.

THE STILL FLAME

The Summit of Silence

Wind. Sky. Stone.

You are standing. You do not remember rising.

The plateau stretches in every direction, dark stone worn smooth by time and weather, open to the sky on all sides. No walls. No path. No summit marker. Nothing that says you have arrived.

Only space.

Your body keeps bracing for impact. Your shoulders stay high. Your weight shifts forward onto the balls of your feet, ready to push, ready to catch—as if the summit might still demand something of you.

But there is nothing to climb.

Your legs twitch with leftover urgency. Your hands drift to your sides and hover there, fingers half-curled, searching for a hold that does not exist.

The mountain has given you everything you demanded—height, distance, the peak above the clouds—and now it gives you the one thing you never asked for.

Nothing to fight.

Your body does not trust it—a shudder, an ache, a suspicion that this is the cruelest trick yet.

You stand very still. Not because you choose to. Because there is nothing left to do.

The wind passes over you, thin and cold, carrying nothing. No voice. No name.

You wait for the next demand.

It does not come.

Minutes pass. Or hours. The sky is pale and uniform, clouds stretched like slow rivers of white, and there is no sun to mark time by.

You realize your jaw is clenched. You release it.

Your shoulders are high and rigid. You lower them—not by deciding to, but because the muscles simply give out, like a rope held too long.

Your hands unclench for the third time in this climb. First in the chamber, by will. Then at the threshold, by surrender. Now—by exhaustion so complete it has become its own kind of permission.

You stand on the summit with your arms loose at your sides, your palms open to the wind, your body swaying slightly like a tree that has forgotten what it is bracing against.

And the spark in your chest does something it has never done before.

It stops flickering.

Not dies. Not dims. It simply—settles. The way a candle flame behaves in a sealed room.

A still flame.

You feel it in your ribs. Not pressing. Not proving. Just there, present, warm, unbothered by the altitude or the wind or the vast indifference of the sky.

It does not need you to move to survive.

It never did.

The knowledge arrives.

Every step since the soil—every reach, every strike, every desperate act of friction—you believed you were keeping the fire alive. You believed that if you stopped, it would go out. That the price of warmth was permanent motion. That you had to earn each breath by climbing toward the next one.

But here, on the summit, you are not climbing. You are not reaching. You are not building or striking or gripping.

And the flame is steadier than it has ever been.

You close your eyes.

What arrives is not peace.

It is the full weight of everything you carried here.

The soil. The pressure. The crack that saved you and the voice that called from below. The wanderer's scarred hands and the fire that burned on without you. The storm. The dead ember. The night you almost chose the snow. The corridor. The figure against the wall. The breath at the eleventh step. The chamber. Your hands in the pool beside hands that were not moving.

It comes all at once—not as memory but as mass. As if every moment you survived has been waiting at the summit, patient, knowing you would have to stand still long enough to feel it.

Your knees buckle.

You do not fall. You lower yourself to the stone, and you sit with your legs folded beneath you, and you press your palms flat against the rock the way you pressed them against the threshold wall, not for grip, but for ground.

Your eyes sting. Your throat closes.

You cry because you are here. And the seed is not. And the climber in the corridor may not be. And the wanderer is somewhere below, building fire again, and the storm is somewhere below, gathering itself again, and the soil is somewhere below, pressing shut again, and you are above all of it, and you cannot help any of it, and the flame in your chest burns anyway.

You sit on the summit and weep for the ordinary cruelty of being alive, that you can carry so much and change so little, that the mountain reveals you and the revelation is not triumph but a kind of holy wreckage.

The wind dries your face. You let it.

After a time, the tears stop. Not because the grief ends. Because the body has a limit, and the limit is a mercy.

You open your eyes.

The sky is the same pale white. The stone is the same smooth gray. Nothing on the summit has changed.

But something in you has become very quiet.

Not the spark—the noise around the spark. The constant hum of effort, of proving, of running from the dark. It has gone silent the way a room goes silent after a door shuts—suddenly, completely—and you cannot remember what the sound was, only that it was there.

In the silence, the flame is very clear.

You look at it. Not with your eyes. With your attention. You feel its edges, its warmth, its rhythm. It's not large. It's not impressive. It's exactly the size it has always been.

But without the noise, it fills the entire space of your chest.

A still flame.

You breathe.

The air is thin but it is enough. It has always been enough. You were the one breathing too fast to notice.

You sit on the summit for a long time. Not meditating. Not reflecting. Not performing stillness.

Just sitting. The way stone sits. The way the mountain itself sits, without apology, without agenda, without the need to be anything other than what it is.

And somewhere in that sitting—you cannot say when—a direction appears.

Not upward.

Not downward.

A turning. Inward and then through—like a compass needle finding north, except the direction it finds is not a place. It is a way of facing.

The way you face when you stop running from the dark and stop chasing the light and simply stand in whatever you are, holding what you hold, owing what you owe.

Your body knows it before your mind can name it. The way your body knew how to open your hands at the threshold. The way your body knew to count heartbeats in the soil.

A direction. Practiced. Chosen. Returned to.

ZYE.

The word does not arrive from outside. It forms the way dew forms, from conditions that were always present, condensing into something visible only when the temperature is right.

You do not say it aloud. You do not need to. It is not a word for speaking. It is a word for turning.

The flame in your chest settles deeper. Not brighter. Deeper.

You sit with it until the sky begins to change.

The pale white darkens by a single shade. The wind shifts. The air cools by a fraction.

Evening is coming, or something like it.

And you feel it—the pull. Not downward. Not the old pull toward the soil.

Toward the world you left.

Toward the corridor. Toward the field where seeds are pressing upward against dirt. Toward the debts your open hands have acknowledged but not yet paid.

You do not want to go.

The summit is the first place since the soil where nothing is trying to bury you. The first place where the flame does not have to fight for air. The first place where your body is not bracing for the next blow.

You could stay. You could sit on this stone and breathe this thin, clean air and let the still flame burn in silence until the mountain takes you back into itself.

The thought is not temptation. It is genuine desire. The deepest rest you have ever felt, offered freely, with no voice whispering "stay" to trick you.

This time, staying would be easy. Staying would be honest. Staying would cost nothing.

And that is how you know you cannot.

Because the flame does not end with you.

It was never meant to.

It is for the corridor. For the field. For every mound of earth where something is pressing upward and does not yet know why.

You stand.

Your legs protest. The summit's stillness has settled into your joints, and your body moves the way a body moves after long prayer, stiff, heavy, reluctant.

You look out from the plateau's edge. And for an instant you feel something above the summit—not height, not sky, but the outline of what you are not yet. A shape you will spend your life approaching and never fill. It does not discourage you. It is the reason the flame wants to move.

Below, far below, the world is hidden in cloud and shadow. You cannot see the valley. You cannot see the path. You cannot see anything except the descent, steep, uncertain, disappearing into gray.

It looks like the soil.

You breathe in. The still flame holds.

You breathe out.

You take the first step down.

The stone tilts beneath you. Your weight shifts forward. Gravity reclaims you—and for the first time since the soil, you do not resist what pulls you down.

And as you descend the first few steps, a strange thing happens: the wind, which has carried nothing but cold all day, carries the faintest warmth across your back, brief, passing, gone before you can be certain it was real.

THE RETURN

The Descent as Ascent

The stone tilts beneath your feet and does not stop tilting.

Within ten steps, the summit is behind you. Not gone, but receding as a breath recedes once the lungs release. The wide plateau narrows back into path. The air thickens. The wind returns in cautious gusts, testing whether your stillness was real or only possible at the top.

Your body answers before you can: your knees ache on the descent. Your ankles roll on loose stone. Your thighs burn in a way they did not burn while climbing, a sharp, burning fatigue that demands patience you are not sure you still possess.

The body does not care that you have been to the summit. It still must be carried.

For a while, the flame holds. Your steps are slow but even. The wind touches your face and you let it. The stone passes beneath your feet and you do not grip.

Then the path steepens. Your knees protest. The fog closes in.

You slip. Catch yourself.

A brief flash of irritation rises: *Be careful. Don't be stupid.*

Old voice. Old tone.

You pause and breathe. Not to punish yourself—to return.

For three steps, you walk angry. You slam your heel harder than necessary. You mutter a quiet insult at yourself—something you have said so many times it has worn a groove in your jaw.

The flame dims. Not gone. Just distant—the way a candle dims when you turn away from it and face the draft.

You stop. Not because you failed—because you noticed.

You turn back toward the flame. Not physically. In the way the summit taught you. The direction that is neither up nor down.

The flame steadies, and you continue.

You pass the smooth wall. The blood is still there, dried dark, already part of the stone.

Cloud thickens below you. The world becomes gray again. Wind sharpens.

A light snow begins to fall—not a storm, but a reminder. The mountain does not forget its weather.

You feel the cold creep into your hands and you remember the night you lost the ember. The memory arrives as a tightening in the chest, a sinking in the stomach—fast, physical, older than thought.

You press your palm to your heart. The still flame answers. Not with warmth. With steadiness.

You keep moving.

The path curves. The ridge drops into a steep descent. Fog gathers until the world is reduced to ten feet ahead.

You move one step at a time. This rock. This breath. This moment.

You descend further. The fog thickens. The path curves back on itself, and for a stretch you cannot tell if you are walking or the mountain is turning beneath you.

And then the stone walls rise on either side.

You recognize it before you see it clearly. Your body tightens. Your stride shortens. Your hands clench at your sides before your mind has caught up to where you are.

The corridor.

You slow.

The walls narrow. The air changes—colder here, trapped, carrying the stale mineral smell of stone that rarely sees wind.

You walk forward. Each step echoes.

You are looking for the place.

You find it.

The spot where the wall curves slightly inward, creating a shallow alcove. The stone there is darker than the stone around it—whether from moisture or shadow, you cannot tell.

No figure slumped against the wall. No body. No bones.

No sign that anyone was ever here at all.

You stand in front of the empty alcove and feel the full weight of not knowing.

They could have risen. Someone else could have stopped. The cold could have finished what you started by walking past.

The mountain keeps no record. The stone tells you nothing.

You press your palm flat against the alcove wall. The rock is cold and smooth beneath your hand. Your split palm, half-healed now, leaves a faint smear—not of blood, but of soot and sweat. A mark that will fade.

The stone is the same temperature as the skin you remember against it—cold, still, open to nothing and everything.

You stand there for a long time.

No voice arrives. No echo. No forgiveness offered or withheld. Just the stone, the cold, and the space where someone was that is now empty.

You cannot undo what you did. You cannot know what it cost.

You can only walk through the corridor and come out the other side carrying the same hands.

You step forward.

The passage opens. The walls fall away. The air widens.

And below you, far below, the valley spreads.

You descend for hours.

The air warms by degrees. The snow turns to cold rain, then to mist. The stone gives way to earth.

The fog thins, and through it—faint, trembling, unmistakable, you hear it.

Not the wind. Not your own breath.

A hum.

Rising from below. From the valley floor. From the place you once rose.

A chorus of quiet pulses, small, buried, persistent—seeds. The same rhythm you counted in the soil. The same hum that found you when you were nothing but weight and will.

You descend faster. Careful, but faster.

The earth softens beneath your feet. The slope levels. The mist parts. And you see them. Not one. Many.

Small mounds in the soil, scattered across the valley floor like a field of sleeping hearts.

The ground trembles. Not from earthquake—from effort. From dozens of small, buried lives pressing upward against the weight of the world.

You approach slowly.

The air here is warmer than the summit, but heavier, thick with longing, thick with fear. The darkness in this valley is not a storm. It is a way of living. You recognize it. You lived in it.

You kneel near the nearest mound.

Your knees press into the same earth you once pressed out of. The posture is the same one you held at the threshold, palms open, weight surrendered, body low.

But the direction has changed.

At the threshold, you knelt to enter.

Here, you kneel to stay.

Beneath the soil, something hears your breath. It does not know what you are. Only that you are warm. Its body aches from pressing upward too many times. Its will is smaller than its fear.

A thought flickers through it, not in words:

Don't make me try again.

Your chest tightens. You have felt this thought. You have been this thought—in the soil, in the storm, in the snow behind the boulders when lying down seemed like the kindest thing the world had to offer.

Voices move through the valley, carried by wind:

Stay buried. It's safer. It's quiet. Don't try. Don't embarrass yourself.

The words are familiar. They were once your own.

Something rises in you—hot, urgent.

You want to dig. You want to plunge your hands into the earth and pull them free. You want to tear the soil apart the way the soil was never torn apart for you—by force, by fury, by the sheer unbearable need to spare someone the pain you carried.

Your hands are already in the dirt. Your fingers are already digging. Soil packs beneath your nails and fills the cracks in your palms.

You are gripping.

The old grip. The one that held the ember too tight. The one that held yourself together so hard you could not open your hands for a stranger in a corridor.

Your fingers close around something beneath the surface—small, trembling, alive.

You could pull.

Every muscle in your arms wants to pull. Every memory of your own burial screams spare them, spare them, nobody spared you.

Your hands tighten.

And then the flame in your chest presses. Steady. Not a warning. A reminder.

You hold everything like that. Stone. Air. People.

The wanderer's voice. Not a memory—a scar, speaking from the grooves in your palms.

You look at your hands in the dirt. Fists again. Clenched around something fragile. Trying to rescue by force what can only be released by patience.

You pulled at the ember and it died.

You gripped your survival and walked past a body in the cold.

You are still the same hands. Still capable of the same closing.

Your fingers loosen. Slowly. Muscle by muscle—the same way they opened in the chamber, at the threshold, on the summit.

You do not pull.

You open your hands and press your palms flat against the earth—the way you pressed them against the threshold stone, the way you pressed one against the alcove wall.

You breathe slowly. You let your warmth pass into the soil without demanding that the soil respond.

The nearest mound trembles harder. A crack forms.

Thin as a needle. Steady as a pulse.

You shift your body so your shadow falls across the crack, blocking the wind. You say nothing.

One small hand breaks the surface, scrapes at the air, and slips back.

You do not reach for it.

Your whole body aches to reach for it. Your arms tremble with the effort of staying still. Staying open. Letting the seed do what you once did—press, fail, press again—without stealing the effort that will teach its hands what your hands learned.

The hand breaks through again. This time it holds.

A forehead follows. A gasp. A cough. The thin, sharp cry of a body meeting air for the first time.

Not victory. Birth.

Across the valley, other cracks form. Other hands press upward. The soil shifts in small avalanches—giving way, reclaiming, giving way again.

Scattered sparks ignite across the field, tiny, fragile, real.

You do not smile like a hero. You smile like someone who remembers what comes next.

They will climb. They will fall. They will face storms and echoes and corridors where someone needs them and they are not sure they have enough. They will lose embers. They will rebuild them. They will grip too hard and learn to open. Or they won't. The mountain will not spare them. But it will reveal them.

You stay where you are, close enough to be felt, far enough not to steal their effort. You breathe where they can hear it.

You rise and look toward the mountain. It stands unchanged, still immense, still inevitable.

Your shoulders are not hunched against it. Your jaw is not set in defiance. Your hands hang open at your sides, palms facing slightly outward, the way they hung when you walked off the summit.

You turn back to the field. To the cracks. To the trembling earth.

Then you notice one mound that has not cracked.

It is smaller than the others. Set apart, near the edge of the valley where the earth is packed harder, where the soil has been pressed tight by stone and old weather.

You walk to it. You kneel.

You press your palm flat against the ground. You wait.

Beneath the surface—faintly, almost too faint to feel—a pulse.

Slow. Unsteady. The rhythm of something that has been pressing upward for a long time and has stopped believing the pressing will lead anywhere.

You wait.

The pulse continues. No crack forms.

You wait longer. The wind moves through the valley. Other seeds are gasping into air, finding light, beginning to stand. The field is filling with the sound of small, astonished breaths.

This mound does not crack.

You stay anyway.

Not because you know it will open. Not because your presence guarantees anything.

You stay because the corridor taught you what leaving looks like, and your hands—your open, scarred, soot-written hands—are not willing to learn that lesson a third time.

You speak the blessing. Quietly. The first words you have spoken aloud since the summit.

"May Zye blossom."

The ground does not answer.

The wind carries the words away, across the valley, over the mounds that have cracked and the ones that have not, past the base of the mountain and into the thin air above.

You stay kneeling. Your knees ache. Your hand is flat on the earth. The cold seeps into your palm.

Beneath your fingers, the pulse continues. Small. Unsteady.

You have felt this rhythm before. In the soil. In the dark. When pressing upward felt like pressing into stone, and the only voice you could hear was the one saying it was not worth the effort.

You press your palm harder into the earth—not reaching, not gripping, just open. The way hands open when the body has finally decided what to carry.

Still there.

THE HUM

When the pages end, the mountain does not.

Listen.

Not for a voice. For the pulse beneath your stillness—

the quiet insistence that lives under breath.

You will feel buried again.

You will feel the old weather return.

The hum will not explain itself. It never has.

But it is there—the way it was there before the crack,

before the flame, before the first breath of open air.

Still there.

May Zye blossom.

GO FOR IT.

GLOSSARY

Terms of Ascent

The Hum — *The sound beneath the silence. It does not explain itself.*

The Crack — *What the dark makes when it is pressed against long enough.*

The Spark — *What catches when friction has nowhere left to go. Fragile. Involuntary. Real.*

Friction — *The cost of becoming. What your hands learn when they refuse to stop.*

The Flamebearer — *One who carries the knowledge of fire in scarred hands. Not the fire itself — the memory of how to build it.*

The Ember — *Warmth made portable. Can be carried. Can be lost.*

The Still Flame — *A flame without wind. What the fire becomes when you stop feeding it with panic.*

The Mountain — *It does not invite you. It does not threaten you. It waits.*

Echoes — *The voices that rise loudest in silence. Some are old weather. Some are debts.*

The Mountain Spirit — *The mountain's inner presence. It does not comfort. It reflects.*

The Threshold — *The place where the mountain asks you to set down what you carried to reach it.*

Stillness — *Remaining without reaching. Not the absence of movement — the end of fleeing.*

Zye /zī/ — *A direction. The practiced return toward light, chosen again and again, before you can prove it is there.*

Ascent — *Not a destination. A repetition.*

Return — *The descent back into the world, carrying what was found. Where what was earned is tested.*

Blossom — *What the pressing was for. Growth made visible through resistance.*

May Zye Blossom — *A blessing spoken into soil that has not yet answered.*

Zyegoat — *The shape you see above the summit. What you are becoming but have not yet become — the pattern the climb reveals, always slightly beyond the arriving.*

Author's Note

This book began in the dark.

Not as metaphor—though it became one. It began in a season where every direction was resistance, and the only movement I could manage was small, ugly, and swallowed by silence.

I didn't write this to teach anyone how to climb. I wrote it because I needed to believe the climb was real—that effort leaves marks even when no one sees them, that the soil can close in again and again but cannot unsplit what has already been opened.

The word *Zye* came to me not as a concept but as a direction—the practiced return toward light, again and again, even before you can prove it is there. I cannot give you that direction. I can only tell you that it exists, and that my hands found it the same way the seed in this story does: by following a hum I could not explain and reaching toward a warmth I was not certain was real.

If you feel buried, I am not above you. I am beside you, pressing against the same weight.

Go for it.

— *Qzye View*

A reading guide for reflection, discussion, and group use
is available at:

zyetopia.com/guides/go-for-it

4

www.ingramcontent.com/pod-product-compliance
Lightning Source LLC
LaVergne TN
LVHW090531110826
845146LV00003B/1059

* 9 7 9 8 9 9 5 4 5 7 5 0 3 *